Or

Esmeray

It's cold in the station tonight.

But it always is this time of year. And yet I still haven't learnt to buy a proper coat. Instead, I'm crouched down by the tracks in my Dell boy style jacket. I fumble around in my drawstring bag for my very outdated, very broken Blackberry and can just about make out the letters on the keypad to unblock my phone, then once I'm in... battery low, followed by a black screen. Great. Guess I never learned to charge my phone either. But I guess when your dad fled the scene at age 8 and your mum lives to get drunk, high and laid every night you never really learn the basics.

And to make matters worse the people at the station Are not much better company.Theyre all probably too drunk to remember their own names.

Platform 3 is now filled with football chants, smashed up bottles and a few too many stern words, derogatory terms and the usual dialect used on a standard Friday night in Salford.

Finally, the train decides to arrive. As I'm about to bored onto carriage Di hear a cry for help in the distance. Followed by an army of helpless passersby suddenly rushing towards the entrance of WHSmith's

I suppose I should go investigate. Or maybe adding another pair of eyes to a person clearly in need will just make matters word. Apparently, I'm good at that.

Ok fine, I clearly have a conscience. I slowly pick up the pace as I barge my way through the crowd of San Miguel scented pedestrians.

"Is someone going to help her or are we all just going to stand here observing?" I hear one of the other ironically observant women in the crowd ask. I give her a stern but confused look as she points to a lady on the ground. "Well?" she says looking at me. "Do something."

In a panic I do as she asks and kneel beside the helpless woman on the ground and throw my bag to the side. With hope in her eyes and an apologetic smile the lady looks at me. "Are you ok?" I ask. The woman in the crowd snickers. "Does she look ok? What a stupid question."

"I'm sorry!" I snap as I turn to face her. "Are your wisecracks really necessary right now or do you have a train to catch?" Thankfully she tuts and walks away and a group of other nosey nobodies follow her.

"Sorry about that." I say to the woman as I take of my coat and let her use it as a cushion. "Can you tell me what happened. The old lady shrugs.

"I only popped in for an ok magazine. "She laughs. "I came outside and my vision just went. Next thing I know I'm laid on the ground with an audience."

"Any pain?" I ask.

She grimaces as she slowly twitches her leg and slightly raises her arm. I search for my bag. Crap it's gone. I sigh as I try not to show any panic on my face but it's no use, she knows.

"Manchester folk, Huh?" She says in derision.

Thankfully a genuinely concerned security guard sees us and informs us that help is on the way.

After about 40 minutes of exchanging pleasantries, we are greeted by two young male paramedics.

"what's your name, Sweetie." he asks the lady. "Audrey." she says short of breath.

"That fall really took your breath away didn't it. Don't worry we will get you sorted. Is your daughter coming too?"

Audreys eyes are suddenly tearful and her head faces the ground. The poor bloke looks at me with eyes struck with foot in mouth syndrome. I give him a reassuring shake of the head as I tell him we just met. The two men escort the lady to the ambulance as I carry her shopping bag and my jacket behind her.

"You're not my daughter, are you? Audrey asks. I can't tell if that tone is relief or disappointment. One of the two is familiar to me. I look at me feet trying to avoid eye contact. "Come on, I need someone to hand feed me humbugs on the way."

I laugh. She needs humbugs? I need two vodka shots and some valium after tonight's antics.

We make our way through the traffic and I can just about make out the billboard signs through my very tired eyes. Suddenly I'm brought back into the room when the paramedic looks up from his laptop after getting Audreys details and he starts asking me questions.

"So, what's your story then?" he asks me.

"How do you mean?" I say perplexed.

"Well." he begins. "you're not her daughter and you said you just met. So, what's a young lady like you doing at the station stone cold sober at this time?"

I rub my forehead as I try to recall the last 24hours.

" Ermm well I finished college, then I ended up being piggy in the middle at rehearsals so I bailed and went for the train. Not that I'm sure where I was heading. Sometimes I start to run before I decide my destination. Then I hear Audrey scream and..." he stops me.

"And she became your destination?" he asks.

I look at Audrey laid on the stretcher. She seems thankful that I'm here.

"I don't know." I say with a smile. "I think that journey has just begun."

Audrey

Here I am again. Laid up in a hospital bed with my name written on a board above my head.

It suddenly dawns on me that I haven't asked the kind young lady her name.

She is kind. I know this because she stayed with me the whole night. Very peculiar. Shes clearly quite young. I wonder why she hasn't left to be with her friends or family. So much to learn yet about this quirky looking character. I chuckle to myself as I watch her fight with the tv to find a channel, muttering a selection of cuss words. Bless her, she must've been raised with a certain level of respect to not swear in front of a pensioner.

She turns back to face me as she's settled for This Morning. She flashes me a smile of relief as she brushes her damp ketchup colored hair out of her face.

The poor girl looks as though she has had a rough night. The circles under her eyes are darker than the black hole of Calcutta, her black nail polish severely chipped and her canvas pumps have seen better days. Did no one ever tell her not to wear such footwear in torrential rain?

"Sorry dear." I say. "Pardon my ignorance, but I never asked your name."

"Oh." She laughs. "It's fine. Erm it's Esmeray."

What a unique name. I knew this girl was intriguing.

"I've never heard that name before does that have a meaning." I ask, waiting for a very long winded, elaborate story.

She shrugs. "Apparently it means princess of darkness."

"Interesting." I reply. This girl appears very reserved I'm trying desperately to understand this girl. Her eyes hold a meaningful stare when she speaks to me. There's a story to tell and it`s hidden behind those hazel eyes, and I'm longing to find it out.

"Shall I get us a brew?" She digresses.

I reach my hand over to gently clasp hers. That must be a hard story to share whatever is. I eagerly accept her offer and request a milky tea with two sugars.

Shortly after Esmeray leaves the room I`m greeted by a young male doctor with mousy brown hair and sparkling green eyes.

"Good morning Mrs. Lane." He says softly. "How are you feeling this morning?"

Shuffling to get comfortable in an upright position I nod at the gentleman.

"I understand." He says in his soft Welsh accent. "You and miss Rose have had quite the experience.

Esmeray Rose? Slowly I'm learning more about her than she probably wishes.

As the doctor explains to me that my blood results and vitals are fine, she returns. Looking at the doctor inquisitively.

He pauses as he does a double take looking at the disheveled girl by my bedside handing me my tea as she takes a sip of her black coffee.

"As I was saying Mrs. Lane." He continues, meeting my gaze once again. "Your vitals and bloods are fine but we need to undergo some more tests as it is possible you have MS."

Esmeray

I stop in my tracks.

Did I just hear that right?

I feel like I've just been submerged into minus degree deep waters.

Why do I feel this sinking feeling for someone I just met?

I look over at Audrey with a concerned look. Damn she has a better poker face than me. If I'd have been given that kind of news id be losing my shit by now.

The doctor goes more in depth about upcoming scans and tests but I'm in too much shock right now to take it in.

He flashes us both a sympathetic smile before he turns to leave.

The poker face is slowly breaking and I can see Audrey trying hard to fight away her tears.

I'm terrible in these situations. I never know how to react. Do I hug her?

"Is there anything I can do for you Audrey?" I ask.

She doesn't look at me. She shakes her head as she picks apart at the fabrics on her bedsheets.

"Don't you have a home to be getting back to? She asks, slowly looking up at me, forcing a smile.

"I guess so." I agree reluctantly. "Listen, I'll leave my number with the staff on the reception desk, call me if you need anything yea?"

I make my way to the bus stop, thankful that the rain has subsided for now. I take a quick glance over my shoulder to look up to Audreys ward. I can't help but feel guilty for leaving her. But it's what she wanted and I can't say I blame her.

I think of her the whole way home. I sit with my knees up on the bus biting the skin on the side of my fingers.

As the bus comes to a sudden holt outside of my shabby council estate, I try to brace myself for what or should I say who I'll be greeted with. I slowly open the door and I'm instantly greeted with the smell of cigarettes and beer cans on the floor.

That can only mean one thing. Mums home.

"OH MY GOD!" I hear her yell as she comes downstairs. "Where on earth have you been."

Where do I even begin? What do I actually tell her?

"Well?" she says standing front of me wither her leopard print blouse hanging off of one shoulder and her signature cigarette perfume. "I've been trying to ring you all night."

"I'm sorry." I begin. "I crashed at Connors and my phone died."

Connor is the bassist in my band. We all call him our hermit. I'm pretty much convinced he doesn't know phones exist. That's why I always use him as an excuse when I disappear, she'll never know otherwise.

"Right well you look knackered." She declares, taking a drag of her Marlborough. "Go on. Go get yourself freshened up; I'll stick a fish pie in the microwave for You."

That being said I run upstairs, fling open my bedroom door and toss my bag onto the bed.

I slump down at my white desk and open my laptop before plugging in my phone and jiggling the wire to get my very broken phone to charge.

A notification flashes on my laptop screen.

11 MESSAGE ALERTS

Great. I disappear for 12hours and Facebook sends out a search party.

Although most of them are probably fake profiles.

Let's see. 3messages from my best friend Lacey asking if I want to go out for cocktails followed by the classic "Bro, you dead?"

Couple of messages from my drummer Adam, asking for an Xbox session.

Wow. Even a concerned message from my so-called boyfriend, Eli.

Of course, that concern is short lived as the following message is him wanting money from me.

Once I've reassured the few people in my life that actually give a damn about me, I drag myself into the shower.

After what feels like the first shower in weeks, I jump into my fresh oversized raiders t-shirt and stranger things Pj shorts and reunite with my mum in the kitchen.

"how've you been mum?" I asked, slowly moving takeaway boxes and outdated letters off of the table.

"What you mean other than worrying about my missing daughter all night, yea great." She smirks, handing me my gourmet meal.

I am so hungry this Tesco's own ready meal looks like the king's finest dish.

I sit quietly whilst I indulge in my meal and observe the kitchen. To the left of the mountain of washing in the sink, I see the boiler blinking at me.

"You didn't call the boiler man did you mum?" I ask trying not to sound too disappointed.

"Oh god!" she says burying her head in her hands, "I knew there was something I forgot to do. I've been swamped babe."

If I know mum at all, I know that's code for I got high and got with Daz from down the road again. Daz is nice in his own little kooky way. Hes about 10years older than my mum, got a dad bod and is basically just existing to keep our house running.

"It's fine." I sigh. "I'll ring Daz, see if I can sort it."

She looks at me relieved. "Ah babe, you're a diamond. Sorry sweetheart I need a lie down."

She staggers off towards the stairs.

"Mum!" I shout after her. "Have you eaten today."

"Uh." she grumbles. "I'll get something later, Darling. Don't worry about me."

I stand in the kitchen watching her struggle to climb the stairs. Shaking my head, I go to the fridge freezer and see what I can prepare for her to eat later.

Typical. Both the fridge and freezer are pretty much bare. Just as I expected.

Looks like a food shop is on the agenda today.

It's coming up to 2pm and the band usually meet at this time every day. Shoot. I'd better get changed. Screw it the t-shirts staying on. I run upstairs and change into some black legging, throw on some odd socks and my blue adidas Giselle trainers. Grabbing my oversized denim jacket and my phone I head down the road to Connors garage. By the time I arrive, everyone is already there, even Eli which is surprising as Hes never usually there.

"Hey there you are." he says bringing me into an embrace. "We thought you was dead."

"Eli!" Lacey says giving him a well-deserved slap on the arm. "Glad you're ok bro." She says reassuringly, giving me a hug.

I swear sometimes she acts more like a boyfriend to me than Eli does.

So, with Connor looking somewhat human on Bass, Lacey on lead guitar and Adam drumming in the back we get to work.

Halfway through teenage kicks I glance over at Eli to see him sat looking very uninterested, scrolling through his socials. Funny. He always says this is our song.

What? I hook up with a guy in the school library at the age of 16 and it haunts you for life. Oh well. But that's how this love story began, and after a year of hook ups I gave him an ultimatum and he chose the relationship lifestyle and were still going strong to this day. Well...maybe not strong, but it's a comfort zone for me.

After about an hour and half of rehearsing we decide to take a break. I check my phone and see I have a missed call from an unknown number. Must be important they left a voicemail. Oh, crap it's the hospital.

"Guys." I say before I even think about what to tell them. Noone knows where I've been all night. And there's no way they'll agree with it or even believe me. "I'm so sorry but I need to go I have somethings to sort out."

"Really? You disappear all night and now you're leaving us again." Connor says, resting his guitar on the stand behind him. It's not like him to be so seemingly annoyed. "Only kidding, you do what you need to, I'm off back to my Call of duty session. Catch you all later." He heads back to his den with his hood up.

Eli looks fuming. Funny how when I'm there he acts like I don't exist but the second I need to leave he's suddenly interested.

"What's so important babe? Something I should be worried about?" Eli says now standing in front of me.

"Eli." I say disappointedly. "Get real, will you? I was out all last night and my mum has got behind on a few things so I need to sort it. Look I'll explain everything to you all later. Just trust me, ok?

He nods with an apologetic look on his face. I give him a quick kiss before heading back to the bus stop and make my way back to Audrey.

I decide to stop off at the Sainsburys on the corner for a few bits for mum. Let's see bread, ham, cheese and some humbugs for Audrey. I have next to no money but at least we can live on Toasties until mums' payment goes in next week.

When I finally get to Audreys room, I see her now sat in the cream leather armchair in the corner. She looks so content.

How is it possible that a total stranger can suddenly feel like home?

Audrey

The vacant expression quickly vanishes from my face when I see that bright, vibrant girl saunter through the door with that big cheeky grin on her face.

"Hey you." She says. "How are you holding up?"

I flash her a sorry smile as I show her the dressing from my previous blood tests.

"Aww man." She says in a seemingly upset tone. "I'm sorry I missed it I had to go home and-"

She pauses. I think she has her own things going on that she clearly doesn't want to share. I bet she feels like it'd be a burden on me because I'm stuck in here.

She really is special. Shes a young girl with her own life and she's here, handing me a bag of humbugs and making the bed before carefully perching herself on it.

I pop a humbug in my mouth and offer her one but she politely declines.

"So?" she starts, looking briefly over her shoulder. "What's been said? The doctor on the phone said you'd had some bloods done."

"Yeah, I'm still waiting for the results back." I explain. "They want me to go for some tests as they think it's MS but they just did blood tests to try and rule out any other possible issues."

After an hour of chatting and trying to guess the right answers on the outdated gameshows that are apparently still running just with new presenters that look like they escaped out of pride and prejudice and ended up in the wrong century, my blood results are still not here. In fact,

I don't remember the last time a doctor or nurse even popped their head around the door to check on me. I'm trying not to get frustrated but Esmeray seems to be a little fed up now as she's began pacing the room.

She then throws her head back and groans loudly in anger. " urrgh what's taking so long." She complains." I understand they're busy but this is taking the pi-"

Before she has time to finish her sentence, she sits back onto the bed but catches the button on the bed remote, causing it to suddenly move down, giving her a fright.

The mood is quickly changed to a more positive one as we both howl with laughter.

All of this commotion has thankfully caused a young female nurse to enter the room.

"You ladies seem to be having fun." the nurse says grinning.

We look at the nurse simultaneously with a relieved expression.

"Oh, thank god." Esmeray calls out, carefully getting back on her feet, giving the bed a stern look after the sudden surprise it gave her. "Any chance of these blood results yet? I'm sorry to be impatient, it's just my friend here has been waiting a long time already."

My heart feels as though it could burst. I have mixed emotions hearing her call me a friend. It's a lovely thing to be called, but for some reason the bond feels more than that.

"Friend.?" the nurse asks. "I'm sorry...only the receptionist told me you were family."

Esmeray laughs, takes a look at me and then suddenly looks concerned.

She looks back at the nurse who suddenly changes her tone. "Oh, my bad. There must have been a misunderstanding. But yes, good news the results are back and the doctor will bring them to you shortly and talk you through the next steps."

I don't know what's going on but I'm not convinced by what the nurse is telling Esme., but I don't want them to worry.

"Not to worry dear." I say reassuringly to the two beautiful girls. "Any chance of a brew?

"Coming up." the nurse says as she exits the room, Esmeray watching her leave before diverting her gaze back to me.

"So?" She smirks. "You like me enough to adopt me, eh?"

This girl makes me laugh.

"Oh, don't be silly dear." I say feeling very confused all of a sudden "That's not possible."

Somethings come over me. I suddenly feel very delirious. I know this girl is familiar, but I have no idea where I know her from. She must be related to me. The only person I know her age is my daughter. That's not my Helen. Is it? I feel emotional. Who is this girl and why is she with me?

Whoever she is, she's looking at me with a very scared look in her eye as she asks me what's wrong.

"I-" I stutter.

Oh no. I can't get my words out. What's wrong with me?

"I don't feel well." I manage to say to the girl." I think you should go home."

The words leave my mouth before I have chance to properly process it in my head.

"What?" She asks. "Are...are you sure I can't help with anything?"

"No!" I snap." I don't need your help. I don't know you."

What have I done? She looks so upset.

Thank God, the nurse is here with the drinks.

"There you go ladies." she says placing the drinks on the table. I look at the girl.

"I'm sorry. " She says. "I have to go,"

And she heads for the door in a hurry. Her long red hair swooping behind her. And just like that, she's gone.

Esmeray

I close the door behind me.

With a tickly throat and blurry eyes, I cover my mouth to muffle the sound of me sobbing.

"Are you ok?" I hear someone say in a familiar accent. I look up to see the good-looking Welsh doctor that saw Audrey when she first came in. He has one hand resting on my shoulder.

"Yea I'm fine. I just need to get back to my mum." I sniff, holding the bag of shopping.

I head for the lift and I hear him call after me. "You know Esmeray." He begins. "We're here for the friends and relatives just as much as the patients."

I turn back to face him and catch his gaze. Those green eyes are weakening.

"Thank you." I say politely. "But I'm ok."

I jump in the lift and I'm about to push the button for the ground floor when I see a family with an old man in a wheelchair heading towards me.

"Room for one more?" he chuckles.

The old man is escorted into the lift by a Lady with beautiful long blonde hair.

I'm still in too much of a daze from the situation with Audrey to understand what he's saying but he seems quite confused and he is not making much sense to me.

"Sorry about my dad." The lady says to me. "He just got his diagnosis for dementia and, well...it's been a long day for us all. "

She's standing next to a very glamourous older woman who is presumably the man's wife. They do all look pretty tired.

"Yeah. That makes too of us." I reply.

As the lift comes to a stop and the doors open on the ground floor, I see a dementia friends' badge on the strap on her handbag resting precariously on her shoulder.

I wonder what that is. Dementia it's always something I've heard about but never looked into it but suddenly I'm very intrigued to learn more.

A short time passes and I arrive home. "Hey mum." I say, kicking off my trainers. "I picked us up some bits from the shop to put us on."

"Ah you're a darling." She beams. "But we don't need to worry about tea tonight. Daz called in to sort the boiler out and he did a chip shop run. That one's yours."

She points towards a small package wrapped in greasy white paper. I start opening it like a starved wolf to find a tray of chips, soaked in vinegar, a few scallops and a small spam fritter.

"Oooh you do spoil us. Thanks Daz." I say stuffing chips in my mouth.

I sit with them for a while and have a catch up whilst we watch a re run of catchphrase before I say my goodbyes and head up to my bedroom, blast out some Avril Lavigne and get to work on my laptop.

I can't get the image of that dementia badge out of my head. Why didn't she say anything? Is it even possible for a person with dementia to know they even, have it?

I definitely need to do my research if I want to continue helping Audrey.

I look up every forum, every support group that google has to offer.

I quickly grab my harry potter notebook and a pen and start making a few important notes.

After a good few hours of research, I feel someone shaking me awake.

I raise my head from my desk to realize there's an excruciating pain in my neck. I must've crashed mid research.

Cautiously, I turn my chair to see who broke my slumber. Of course. It's Eli.

"Eli." I say, trying to disguise the pain in my neck. "What are you doing here."

That question answers itself rapidly as he begins kissing my neck. I laugh as I push him away and rub my eyes before quickly shutting my laptop."

"Ok what's the deal?" He asks.

I give him a puzzled look as he shakes his head and paces the room.

"Somethings not right with you Esme." he continues. "Noone has hardly seen you for the past week or so, and when they do see you, you're so vacant! Then you rush off to God knows where. And now I'm here trying to-"

I jump to my feet in utter disbelief "what?" I say stopping him in his tracks. "Trying to what Eli? Get the one thing from me that you want? Well, I am sorry Eli but there's more important things in my life right now than sex."

He stares at me in profoundly.

"Don't bullshit me Es." he says curtly. "What's so important? You couldn't care less about college, your mums taken care of with Daz, she doesn't need you. Me Esmeray, I need you. The band needs you. We should be your main focus. What's suddenly so important in your life that you've forgotten us?"

No Esmeray. I Tell myself, no. Don't you dare show him weakness and cry in front of him. Not a chance.

I take a breathe. "I." Oh god, I'm choking on my words as my eyes fill with tears."I can't tell you."

He gives me a look I know all too well. "Esme?" he stutters "Is there someone else?"

Oh, if only he knew. Technically there is but not in the way he's suggesting.

I laugh a nervous laugh. "I'm not cheating on you if that's what you mean."

How could he even suggest such a thing? Although, with my sudden change in behavior I can sort of see where he's coming from.

The realization slowly washes over me that I have to tell him what's been happening. I tell him the full story of how I was at the train station to come home after college and how I saw Audrey in need of help.

I tell him the whole story in baited breath. The glint in his eyes tells me Hes not buying it.

He perches on the side of my bed. "So that's why you've been so distant to help someone you barely know?" He grills me.

"What was I supposed to do Eli? She had no one. I need to be there for her." I ask.

"I don't know." he says walking slowly back over to me. "But what I do know is I am your boyfriend, the band they're your friends and weve all been pushed aside for some pensioner."

Ok. Maybe I haven't known Audrey that long but these words are cutting me deep like a knife.

I'm really struggling to keep my tears back so I turn away from him.

"Well." I choke. "If that's how you feel maybe you should just go."

No way I could've said that whilst looking into his eyes.

"Fine." He laughs in disbelief.

I hear the door slam and just like that he's gone.

Audrey

I'm woken up suddenly to the sounds of emergency buzzers going off across the ward.

Blurry eyed and a little nauseous I sit up in my hospital bed trying to figure out what all the buttons on the remote mean.

Honestly, you'd need a degree to figure this thing out.

The young doctor appears just in time and sits me up using that magic remote.

We both laugh at my stupidity. Although I know in his profession, he won't see it that way.

Something feels a little off this morning but I can't quite put my finger on it.

I feel confused and somewhat irritated.

Why can't I remember what happened yesterday?

Instantly I point the blame to any medications they've probably fed me.

"How are you today, Audrey." He asks with that gentle smile.

I don't want to worry the poor chap. So, I tell him I'm fine. "I could murder a coffee though if you have a minute."

He flashes a sympathetic smile before agreeing to my request. "Coming right up."

I keep watch of the door as he leaves.

It's odd. It's almost like I'm waiting for someone to arrive. But who could it be?

A young family come in with gifts for the old man sitting opposite. He's a lucky man, Hes showered regularly with biscuits, flowers and some old books and movies.

A glamourous looking lady who looks about my age makes her way carefully to the TV and slips in a disc.

Wait a minute.

I recognize this film. That's quite rare in here.

Yes. I remember. It's a film I used to watch when I was younger with my Helen.

The king and I.

This is quite refreshing. To say I've not been able to remember much about the last 24hours, I remember this film pretty much word for word.

As I'm having a duet with the gentleman across the room to 'Getting to know you,' the young DR returns with my coffee.

"Having fun?" He beams "Well I'm sorry to crash the party but I've been informed that you can have your scan this afternoon if you're ok with it?" he says passing me my coffee.

I'm not sure if I'm relieved or nervous. Maybe a bit of both. But I agree to it.

"Excellent. You can eat before the scan as it isn't for another 6hours." He explains.

"Ooh excellent." I reply. "I'll have avocado and poached eggs on toast."

Thankfully, the whole room picks up on the blatant sarcasm and they all burst into laughter.

"Don't look so scared dear. "I tell the doctor." I'll have the usual, porridge and jam."

Once again, he disappears and I'm still fixated on the door in case I get a visitor.

I head down for my MRI scan.

The doctor has clearly done his research on me. One of the activity coordinators wrote an all about me form during a one-to-one session with me the other day and asked what my favorite artist was. I told her it was Shirley Bassey, and in the background, I can hear Diamonds are forever.

Suddenly I'm taken back to a time I could never forget.

This was the song I sang at the local church when I met my husband many moons ago.

He was propping up the bar during a church event. The one local to me had them all of the time and I decided to perform that song with a few good friends.

The moment I started singing, he turned around and held his gaze for the whole song. Once I'd finished, I walked over to him as bold as brass and introduced myself. Of course, phones didn't exist in those days so we exchanged addresses and spent the next few weeks being each other's pen pals.

As I begin to recall this memory I suddenly remember more of that story. How I used to work on cruise ships, I was the entertainment every night on cruises across the globe. Then one day I looked out into the audience and there he was again, Arthur, my now late husband.

The mri ends whilst I'm lost in thought. I sit myself up slowly with a tear in my eye.

The handsome young doctor escorts me back to my ward, and I see there's another bunch of flowers. But this time they're for me. Who would've been kind enough to bring me flowers? Is it my Helen?

I walk slowly to my chair next to my bed and there's a familiar young girl sitting there.

"Look who came back to see you." The doctor says "Esmeray."

"Esmeray?" I say puzzled. "That's an unusual name. I haven't heard that before."

The young girl and the doctor give each other a slightly disappointed look.

"Why the flowers dear?" I ask.

"Well." She says with a soft smile. "Il thought it'd cheer you up. I know its been difficult for you being stuck in here. Do you remember I brought you into the hospital?"

I look at her with a look of pure appreciation. I might not know this girl, but from her kind eyes and thoughtful gestures I know she cares.

"Did you?" I ask. "Thank you, dear. And thank you for the flowers they're beautiful."

She stands up to let me take a seat as she exits the room with the doctor and I settle back into chair and exchange pleasantries with the gentleman sat across from me, still with his family.

Esmeray

I close the door and turn to the young doctor, who by looking at his name badge I have now discovered is called Riley.

"So?" I ask." How has she been?"

He gives me a smile. " Well." He starts, standing arms crossed. "She had her MRI today so we need to wait for the results to come back before we can let her go. WE have also managed to get hold of her medical records but haven't been able to get hold of her family. But good news is we now know where she lives."

"That's great!" I cheer. "And where's that exactly."

"Rochdale." He says looking less hopeful. "Quite a while away from here. And with no family, I'm not sure how possible it'd be for her to go home."

My heart sinks. "Because of her Ms.?" I ask.

"Well yes, as her MS progresses it will make it difficult for her to mobilize herself and complete daily tasks." He stutters. "But that's not all. Her medical records show she has been diagnosed with Alzheimer's in the past."

I knew it!

It's difficult to take in. But at least I have an idea of how to help her now.

"So, what happens now?" I ask.

"Well." He shrugs." If we can't get in touch with any family members, shell be looking at needing carers, potentially moving into a care home."

A heart sinking feeling runs through me like a Tidalwave.

I've really become fond of Audrey; I feel like for someone I've just met she understands me better than anyone.

"Is there no way of contacting her family?" I ask.

He looks disheartened. "Her daughter, Helen is her next of kin, but she's been impossible to get hold off." He explains. "My guess is that she's changed her contact details and not updated them on her Mothers GP systems.

"But don't we need to consult her family before making decisions on Audreys behalf?" I say inquisitively.

He chuckles out of clear amazement at how invested I am in Audreys situation. "Well Audrey has what's known as fluctuating capacity, which means in some cases she's aware of the situation she's in, consequences and danger that can occur as well as making some decisions. She appears to be in the early stages of dementia at the moment but we can never assume anything in this job."

He sees the look of stress on my face as I wonder what to do to help her and places a hand on my shoulder,

"For the time being, all we can do is try and remind her of her life before she came here." He says, handing me a sheet of paper. It's the activity she's been doing with the coordinator and it's titled 'All about me.'

Just reading it tells me everything I need to do to trigger a memory for Audrey.

I take a seat outside of her ward and begin to read as Riley gets back to work:

I love learning about her history, but I need to learn more. I have a few ideas of how to bring back some memories for Audrey.

All I want to do right now is go and discuss them with my boyfriend, but Hes undoubtedly mad at me for reasons only he can explain.

I make a mad dash for the lift and decide to go and make up with Eli

A short time passes because for once the buses have been reliable.

Eagerly I make my way to his front door and press the door-bell. Gosh I can hear the dulcet tones of the doorbell from here.

He opens the door looking a little flustered, and shirtless. I look at him confused.

"Esmeray, I didn't expect to see you so soon after our last conversation." He says, looking rather shocked.

"I know," I begin as I make my way through the door and pace his living room. "I just don't like to leave things unresolved and after everything I told you about Audrey, I've had some ideas on how to help her but I feel bad for you feeling neglected about me. I still love you."

As I'm talking, I can hear the sound of a glass breaking in the kitchen behind me, then I realize why he looked so surprised to see me. Also, I realize why he answered the door in only his adidas joggers.

"You're not alone are you." I quiver.

There's a brief moment of silence. He has no reply, we just hold a gaze that says more than any word in the English dictionary ever could.

I quickly turn around and fling the door open and I stand in utter disbelief at who's stood in his kitchen quickly sweeping up the broken glass looking rather scantily clad.

"Oh my god." Are the only words I can force out. "Lacey?"

Wow. You have one disagreement with your boyfriend and he jumps in bed with your best friend. I look at Eli hoping there's some magical chance that I'm dreaming this entire scenario. Still, he has no words. I can't breathe. I make my way to the door but he follows me halfway up the driveway.

"Come on Esme lets sort this." He says.

"That's ok, you have another mess to attend to." I reply, referencing the broken glass in the kitchen but to be honest, he can take from that statement what he will.

For the first time in a very long time, all I want is my mum. That being said I make my way home.

As I walk up to the front door, I notice Daz's car outside. I'm too overwhelmed to care at this moment in time. She could have the whole street in our little home and I probably wouldn't even notice.

I have the heaviest heart when I see my mum stand up from the sofa as I walk in. I manage to muster the word Mum before flinging my arms around her and hugging her tightly and sob uncontrollably on her shoulder.

I tell her everything as I'm laid on the sofa with my head resting on her lap as she brushes my hair like she used to do when I was little, before she adopted drugs in her life. I tell her all about Audrey and how Eli has been a complete tool about the whole thing.

There's a silence.

Slowly I sit upright and dry my eyes.

I look at her for the first time after relaying everything back to her and a look of pride washes over her face.

"Oh love." she sighs.

She seems pleasantly surprised that I've actually opened up to her about my life. I never usually do that. Normally when something bothers me, I lock myself away in my room and blast out the heaviest music I can think of.

I glance over at Daz, finally realizing I've just had a full-on breakdown in front of him. "I never liked that coward." He says taking a sip of his lager

Mum wipes a tear from my eye and reassures me that things will work out and that Eli is a few unholy words that I'm too hurt to resonate with.

"For the record Es." She starts again. "I think you're a very brave and smart young lady and I know whatever you decide to do for Audrey will be in her best interest."

As I sit with them and watch Shirley valentine, I start to feel better. I share stories with them about Audreys history on the cruise ship.

Just at that moment, the film finishes and an advert begins.

I lean forward in awe at what I'm seeing.

It's an advertisement about a programme for apprenticeships on a cruise ship specializing in care work for elderly people with multiple health problems. Apparently, you can learn all about the care industry whilst being a live in carer for those in need.

What better way to bring back some memories for Audrey, than for her to be on a cruise ship taking part in activities with people of a similar age to her with their own problems that will also be taken care of.

I immediately take out my phone and make a note of the details of the cruise programme and submit my application.

What's more reassuring is that I know the cruise ship tailors to people with M.s and I know this because the name of the boat is called Orange Ribbon.

When I did my research following her diagnosis, I found out that the orange ribbon is the support ribbon for people suffering with M.s

On that note I think it's time to call it a day and get myself of to be.

I give my mum and Daz a big hug and thank them for their support before making my way to my bedroom with an overwhelming feeling of hope.

Not only am I making a life for myself but it'll be a great experience for Audrey too.

Audrey

I'm woken abruptly to a girl standing over me and the same feeling of confusion as before.

Shes calling my name and shaking me awake.

She seems different today but I'm not sure why.

I feel the familiarities as she's standing there with a smile and flowers. Stood next to her is a smartly dressed young man who I can only assume is the doctor.

The pair help me to sit up in my bed and hand me a cup of tea. "Mum." The girl says. "It's me, Helen."

Why was I not expecting that name?

Just then another figure comes through the door and introduces himself to the couple sat beside my bed.

"Hi you must be Audreys daughter." He says in that familiar friendly tone. "I'm Riley the doctor. I've been taking care of your mother for the past couple of weeks."

She looks at him with gratitude. "Thank you. This is my Husband, Gregg. "She says pointing to the smart dressed man beside her. "Sorry to ask, but where's the other flowers come from? Has my mum had another guest?"

The doctor explains that a girl brought me here and has been checking on me regularly whilst my family has been unable to. "I think that's why she was a little confused when she saw you when she woke up this morning. "He explains. "The thing with dementia, is when you have it you recognize certain attributes but can't always identify different people. See, Audrey has been used to seeing me and Esmeray, so she's remembered a male and female visiting her regularly but can't always remember their names or even realize the difference in appearance or age."

By the look on Helens face I think she's beginning to understand my diagnosis.

"So, this girl, Esmeray." She questions the nurse. "She found my mum at the station and brought her in? And has been visiting her regularly."

He gives her a reassuring nod of the head. "That's correct."

Just then, Esmeray walks through the door, with a small pile of papers in her hand. Sheepishly she makes her way over to us and introduces herself.

Helens giving her a bit of a stern stare which makes her feel uncomfortable, I think.

She starts to Interrogate her about her background and her bond with myself.

Esmeray catches Helen up on everything that's happened with me recently, my recent diagnosis for M.s and my dementia progression.

She hands Helen the papers.

"I'm glad I've got the chance to meet you, Helen." She says. "I found this programme last night and I think it would be a really good opportunity for your mum to get the care she needs as well as develop some new skills myself."

Helens stern look turns more sour. "You're kidding right?" She barks. "You want me to let my mum go on a cruise with a stranger?"

"Oh, come on Helen." I step in. "She's no stranger. I know I'm not exactly great at remembering anyone at the best of times but I do know I have something good with this girl and she clearly cares and I'm grateful for that."

Gregg stands up and places his hands on Helen's shoulder "You know babe." He says softly. "It might not be such a bad idea."

She spins around to face him, quick enough to shake his hands off of her.

"Who's side are you on? She snaps. "We've just found out my mums in hospital, flown halfway across the world to see if she's ok and now I'm expected to just let her go off with a girl we just met."

"Well, it was just a suggestion. I submitted an application but haven't been accepted yet." Esmeray explains.

Riley looks at Esmeray with a reassuring grin. "Oh, don't sell yourself short. You've already been an excellent carer to Audrey." He continues.

I take a slight glance at Helens face and if I know my daughter, I'd say she's slowly coming round to the idea of leaving me in Esmeray's care.

Helen sighs. "How old are you, Esmeray? Don't you have college or something?"

Esmeray rolls her eyes and sighs deeply. " Oh, that." She scoffs. She shakes her head with tears in her eyes. "I do go to college; I've been studying music but we've broken up for half term at the moment but honestly my hearts not really set on going back."

I reach my hand out to hold hers. My heart is full of love for this girl. She's been like my second daughter.

Helen stands arms folded, facing Esmeray. "Music?" She scolds."Youre studying music?"

"What's wrong with that?" Esmeray asks.

"Well it's hardly a life goal is it?" Helen says belittlingly.

"That's enough Helen." I snap. "Give the poor girl a break. She's on half term break and has spent the majority of that time with me, taking care of me. Is that enough of a life goal for you? Someone her age, looking after your mother whilst you were busy chasing your dreams?"

"Music is the only thing I'm good at." Esmeray adds. "I've been made aware that my mum doesn't need me, never planned on being a mother and clearly im a shitty girlfriend or else my boyfriend wouldn't have got off with my bestfriend. So I'm clearly not good enough as a friend to anyone either so maybe being your mums carer is my only real purpose."

I turn away to dry my tears.

I give her hand a tight squeeze then look back at Helen and Greg.

"Why don't you give me and Helen a chance to talk alone." I say softly, politely asking everyone else to leave the room for a while.

They all exit the room and close the door and I give Helen the classic mum look.

"What is your problem exactly?" I begin. "That girl has a heart of gold. She missed her train to bring me in here, visited me pretty much every day and really took care of me. She knows this experience will be good for me but it will also be a fresh start for her to do something good. All she ever wanted to do was to make her mum proud, make herself proud and find a purpose in this messed up world."

Helen sits beside me and burst into tears.

"Oh love." I say sympathetically. " What is it? What are you afraid of?" I stroke her hair.

She buries her head in her hand and shakes her head.

"It's not that." Helen sobs." I just feel guilty. That girls known you five minutes and has already put more effort in than me. It should be me giving up everything to be with you."

"Don't feel guilty Darling." I add. "You've done plenty for me before you moved away. You hosted every Christmas, drove me places I needed to be, visited me every week for Sunday dinner. The list goes on. Now this girl wants a turn. So take it as a break. We will still keep in touch, love. And you'll always be my first-born Daughter. Noone can replace that."

Helen sits upright and smiles at me. She holds both my hands in hers. "Well then. " She sniffs. " I guess it's decided then."

Esmeray

1 Missed Call.

That's weird.

Noone ever phones me.

And this is from an unknown number.

Well they didn't leave a voicemail so it can't have been important.

I shove my phone back under my pillow and turn over.

Just then, it rings again.

I sit up frantically and answer it.

"Hello?" I answer in a very sleepy tone.

"Good morning." They reply. "Am I speaking to Miss Esmeray Rose?"

"Errm yes, that's me. Who is this please?" I ask.

"This is Sarah, I work in recruitment for the orange Ribbon programme. I received your application and would love to invite you for a face-to-face interview." She explains.

I jump to my feet, stunned for words.

"Oh my gosh!" I stammer. "That's amazing!"

"I'm glad you think so." She adds. "All we need to do is have this interview, just so I can get to know you and then review your sponsored client. Audrey, is it?"

"Yes, that's correct." I say, finally managing to string a sentence together. "Brilliant, when can we do the interview?"

"Wow." She chuckles. "You are intrigued, aren't you? How about this afternoon?"

"That would be perfect." I beam.

We agree to meet at 2pm, it's currently 9am and I have work to do.

I run downstairs to find mum crashed on the sofa, probably on a come down from whatever drugs she spent the night with.

"Mum." I yell shaking her awake. "Mum, I need your help, wake up."

Usually that works, but she seems more out of it this morning.

I scan the room and I see a needle on the table next to multiple empty cans

Shit. Today of all days. This is just like my mum.

Without thinking I run barefoot out of the door down the street and bang on the door at Daz's house.

He opens it looking weary eyed and still in his pajamas too.

I burst into tears when I see him.

"I think mums overdosed she won't wake up." I sob.

His face is as white as a sheet.

"Ok Es." He says, pulling on a salmon-colored hoodie. "Try to stay calm come on let's go."

I head back up the street whilst calling 999, Daz is a few feet behind me, trying to walk whilst putting on his trainers.

We get back into the house and mum still hasn't moved.

"Mum. Can you hear me?" I say, still on the phone to the ambulance.

They ask me a series of questions about her current situation and a bit about her history. I tell them about as much as I can, though I don't know much about what's happened.

Help is on the way. I'm sat on the floor next to the sofa where she's laid.

Daz is sat next to me trying his best to comfort me.

"I've failed her again." I say to him. "I have an interview this afternoon but how can I leave her like this."

"Come on kid none of this is your fault. Your mum needs help and hopefully now she can get that." He says, pulling me closer. "You get yourself ready for the interview, I'll stay with your mum."

A short time passes and the ambulance arrives and checks her over before hoisting her onto a stretcher and helping her into the ambulance.

I quickly run upstairs and throw on a smart casual outfit and jump into the ambulance with them. I have to do this.

"What about your interview?" Daz asks.

"I have a few hours yet." I sigh. "I can come with her and then still make it in time for the interview, it's only 15minutes away."

We arrive at the hospital and we're stuck in the waiting room, in a small cubicle.

Mums checked in and hooked onto a drip to drain out the drugs she's taken.

I sit watching the clock but it doesn't seem to be moving.

Printed in Great Britain
by Amazon

16277330R00031